Atlantic

G. Brian Karas

PUFFIN BOOKS

PUFFIN BOOKS
Published by Penguin Group
Penguin Young Readers Group,
345 Hudson Street, New York, New York 10014, U.S.A.
Penguin Books Ltd, 80 Strand, London WC2R ORL, England
Penguin Books Australia Ltd, 250 Camberwell Road, Camberwell, Victoria 3124, Australia
Penguin Books Canada Ltd, 10 Alcorn Avenue, Toronto, Ontario, Canada M4V 3B2
Penguin Books (N.Z.) Ltd, 182-190 Wairau Road, Auckland 10, New Zealand

First published in the United States of America by G. P. Putnam's Sons,
a division of Penguin Putnam Books for Young Readers, 2002
Published by Puffin Books, a division of Penguin Young Readers Group, 2004

13 14 15 16 17 18 19 20

THE LIBRARY OF CONGRESS HAS CATALOGED THE G. P. PUTNAM'S SONS EDITION AS FOLLOWS:
Karas, G. Brian. Atlantic / G. Brian Karas. p. cm.
Summary: Explore what the Atlantic Ocean is, how far it stretches, how the moon
affects it, and other characteristics as described by the ocean itself.
ISBN: 0-399-23632-5 (hc)
[1. Atlantic Ocean—Fiction. 2. Ocean—Fiction.]
I. Title.
PZ7.K1296 At 2002 [E]—dc21 2001019602

Puffin Books ISBN 978-0-14-240027-2

Manufactured in China

To the Gideons—
David, Priscilla, Derek, Gwenn and Roan

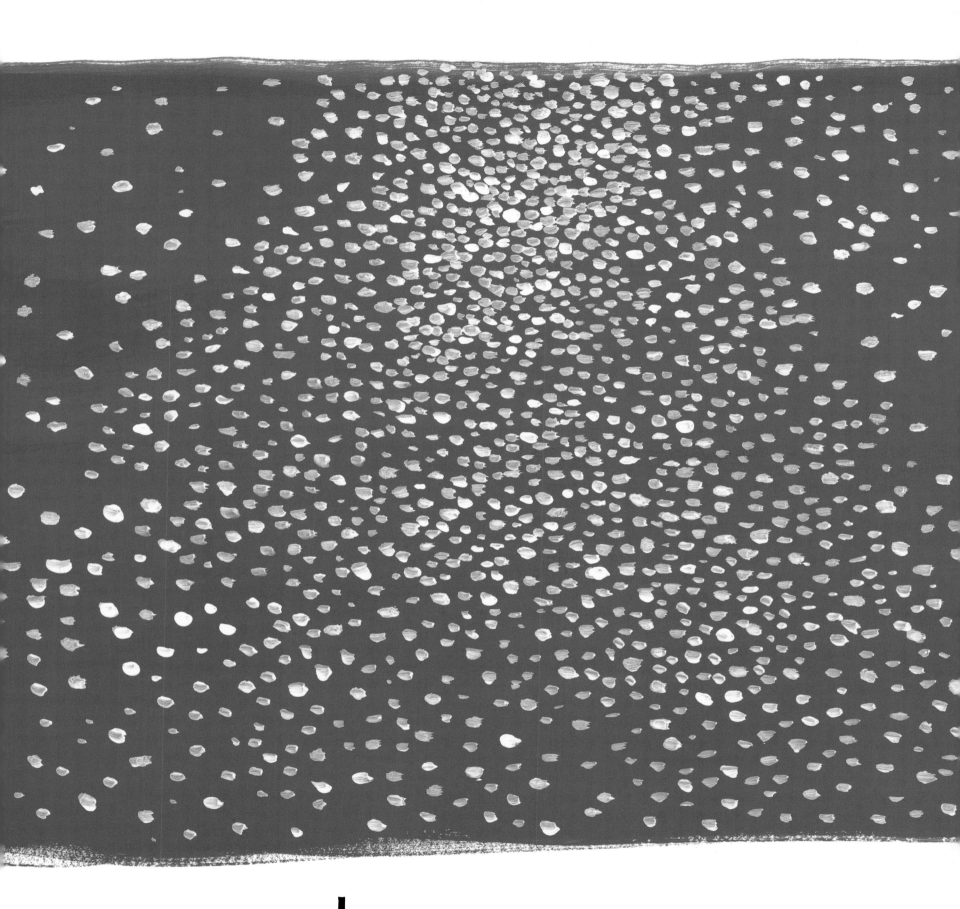

I am the Atlantic Ocean

I begin where the land runs out
at the end of yards
and streets
and hills

I am the blue water at the beach,
the waves,
mist and storms
That salty smell is me too

I stretch from the icy poles,
  North and South
I rub shoulders with North America
  and bump into Africa
I slosh around South America and crash into Europe

But I don't end there
The Pacific and Indian,
Arctic and Antarctic
are my relatives
We are one big family

My water doesn't stay in just one place   It travels from continent to continent

So that iceberg floating past someone's window one day

will sometime find itself lapping at your toes on a warm, sandy beach

My fingers stretch out
Bays and inlets reach far into the land
Gulfs, seas, sounds and channels
        lead to me
            and into me
They are me

I am here day and night,
heaving,
        raging,
                lying still
scraping away at some land
        and putting it someplace else,
                bit by bit
My shape changes,
        as it has for ages
sometimes growing,
        sometimes shrinking
                never staying still

The sun
  so many millions of miles away
   heats my water,
 which turns into clouds and storms
  that rain into me
    and it starts all over again

The moon
so far out in space
pulls at me
and then lets go
so my tides go in and out,
ebb and flood

First I was discovered
(even though I was here first)
and then conquered
by men in big ships
who named me
I've been crossed and probed,
charted,
studied,
dirtied

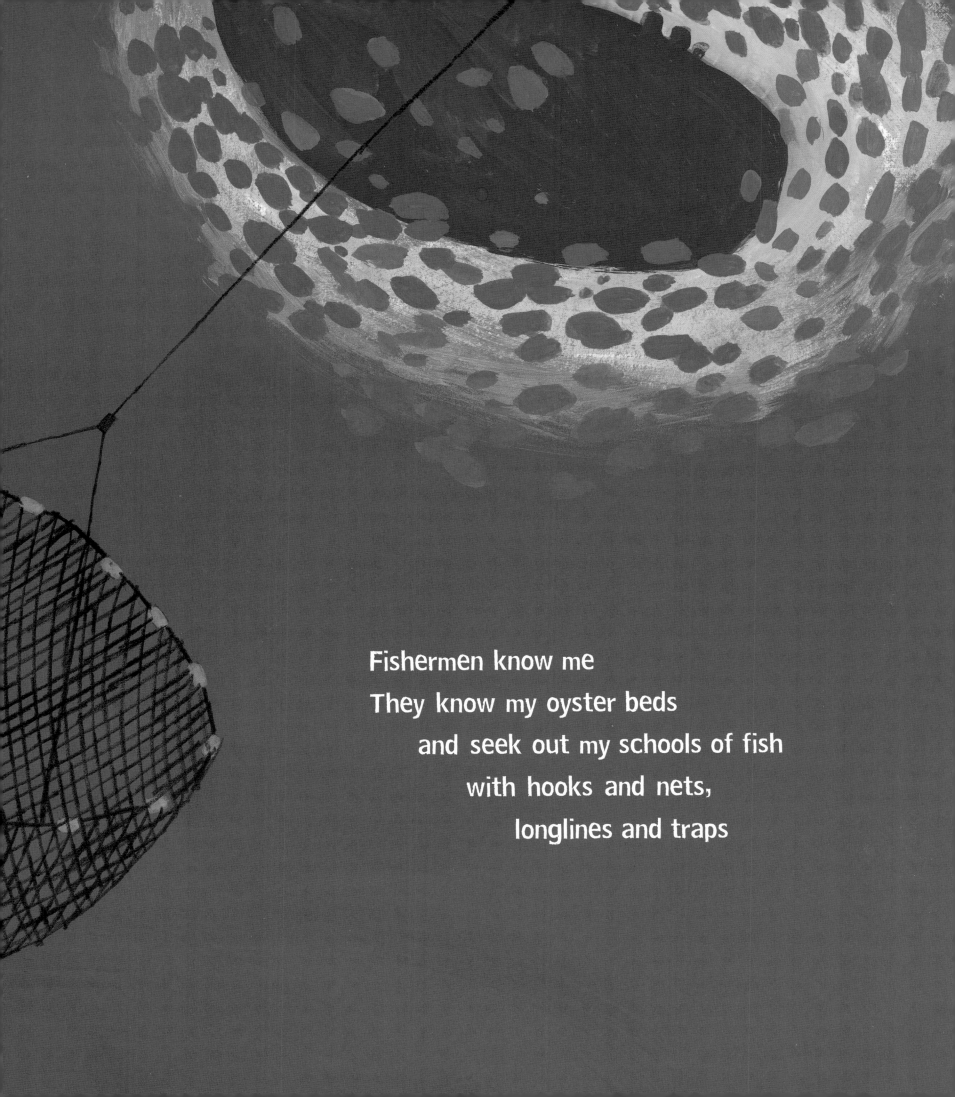

Fishermen know me
They know my oyster beds
    and seek out my schools of fish
      with hooks and nets,
        longlines and traps

So is this great and wide sea, wherein are things creeping in

is found again. What? Eternity. It is the sea Gone with the sun

yron And Spanish sailors with bearded lips, And the beauty

ak, break, break, On thy cold, gray stones, O sea! *Alfred, Lord Tennyso*

riad laughter of the ocean waves. *Aeschylus* Who can number th

straits; A pleasant walk, A pleasant talk, Along the briny beac

Little drops of water, Little grains of sand, Make the mighty o

I call to the earth and sea half-held b

Artists paint pictures of me
with cerulean,
cobalt and ultramarine

...erable, both small and great beasts. *the Holy Bible* Oh sou...

...thur Rimbaud I have bathed in the poem Of the Sea... *Arthur Rim...*

and majesty of the ships, And the magic of the sea. *Henry*

Ocean, who is the source of all. *Homer* All the rivers run

and of the sea, and the drops of rain, and the days of eterni...

Lewis Carroll The sun was shining on the sea, Shining with all h...

...n And the pleasant land. *Julia A. Fletcher Carney* The sea is calm

...he night. *Walt Whitman* And alone d... ...ever The kings of the

And poets know me with their beautiful words

The dancing shadow of your airplane

skips over wave over wave

with dolphins who sing and race
with skates and whales and fish that fly

Seagulls sing to me
Sand and pebbles
    rattle and clatter a chorus
    as I rush in
        and pull away

My words crash and whisper in your ear

Don't forget I am here

I am the Atlantic Ocean

Some Things About Me

I am not the earth's largest ocean, that's the Pacific. But I have many miles of shoreline because of my inlets, bays, gulfs, seas, sounds and channels. Some people think of all the earth's oceans as one, the World or Global Ocean.

If you were to empty me of all my water, you would find deep trenches (the Puerto Rico Trench is 8,648 meters deep—you could fit Mount Everest in the Puerto Rico Trench and only a little bit would stick up), wide basins and the earth's longest mountain range, the Mid-Atlantic Ridge.

I move about in giant currents, like the Gulf Stream and the Brazil and North Atlantic Currents, bringing warm weather to Ireland and dry winds to Africa.

I have been around for ages. Though I am from millions and millions of years of rain, I am the earth's youngest ocean. In the beginning the earth had one ocean, the Panthalassa.

I continue to grow, a couple of inches wider each year. What will I look like 200 million years from now, I don't know.

But for as old as I am, and as strong as I can be, I am in danger. What doesn't belong in my water are chemical and people wastes, oil and garbage. Please treat me with respect!